The Companion

P. ⟨signature⟩

The
COMPANION

A Novella

PAD BROTHERTON

NEW YORK

LONDON • NASHVILLE • MELBOURNE • VANCOUVER

The Companion

A Novella
© 2019 Pad Brotherton

Published in New York, New York, by Morgan James Publishing. Morgan James is a trademark of Morgan James, LLC. www.MorganJamesPublishing.com

The Morgan James Speakers Group can bring authors to your live event. For more information or to book an event visit The Morgan James Speakers Group at www.TheMorganJamesSpeakersGroup.com.

ISBN 9781642790870 paperback
ISBN 9781642790887 eBook
Library of Congress Control Number: 2018943613

Cover Design by:
Christopher and Heather Kirk
www.GFSstudio.com

Interior Design by:
Chris Treccani
www.3dogcreative.net

In an effort to support local communities, raise awareness and funds, Morgan James Publishing donates a percentage of all book sales for the life of each book to Habitat for Humanity Peninsula and Greater Williamsburg.

Get involved today! Visit www.MorganJamesBuilds.com

To My Companion

*Call to me and I will answer you and
tell you great and unsearchable things
you do not know.*
—Jeremiah 33:3

Chapter 1

*I wondered if that was how forgiveness
budded; not with the fanfare of
epiphany, but with pain gathering its
things, packing up, and slipping away
unannounced in the middle of the night.*
—**Khaled Hosseini,** *The Kite Runner*

I can't take my eyes off the pink, marble-glazed
alpenglow cast across the high mountains in
the background. I am so transfixed that I don't
notice we're turning until my driver pulls the
vehicle in a sharp correcting turn down the
hidden lane. Though the hard rain had stopped
an hour earlier, the still-muddy and pitted road
has me jostling about in the backseat of the

taxi until, three-quarters of a mile on, I spot the small chalet upon the reach.

"Pull up here," I tell the driver as I point to a clearing in front of the home. Slinging my backpack over one shoulder, I pay the pudgy man and remind him to return for me in twelve hours.

The mud sucks with my every step toward the dimly lit home, and I wonder why I wore my good loafers to travel to this godforsaken place. The thought also crosses my mind that the residents might not be home, but relief washes over me when I see a shadowy figure in the window. Before I can even curl my knuckles to knock on the plain wooden door, the stubble-haired resident cracks it open about six inches.

"Nils Roser?" I inquire.

Nodding his head up and down, he pushes the door open to allow me in from the January cold.

I can barely make out the words spoken in his thick French accent as he turns his back to me.

"Hang your things on the peg and remove your shoes. Then come with me."

I can follow instructions well enough, but I'm already feeling the same chill that I'd experienced during my entire journey from the airport in Sion. The fifteen-hour flight from Denver to Geneva, Switzerland, is starting to take its toll. Bone-weary, I splay my swollen toes inside my socks with each step toward the back of the small home.

The dark and narrow hallway gives way to a wide-open living area, and the view out of the floor-to-ceiling windows immediately draws my eyes. It's now past dusk, yet I can still make out the dramatic mountain backdrop. My attention to nature is cut short and my feet stop moving when I see Nils standing behind a woman with his hands on her shoulders as she is seated at the dining room table, looking back at me.

"Mr. Westfall, this is my wife, Linn."

"Yes," I say to Linn, "There's no doubt you're Libby's twin. The resemblance is uncanny. Nice to finally meet you."

Nils urges me to sit down and offers to get me something to drink. Seeing that they both have mugs at their places, I mumble something about appreciating whatever they have available.

While her husband makes the short trip to the kitchen, Linn holds out her hand to shake mine before I take my seat across from her. She seems friendly enough, even though Libby had given me more than ample warning about the strained relationship she has with her sister.

"Mr. Westfall—"

"Will. Please call me Will."

"Will it is, then. I'm quite curious as to why you would make such a long trek to this country in the dead of winter from Colorado to see me. I know that my sister sent you, but I can hardly imagine why she'd send a complete stranger to deliver whatever message she has for me."

"I'm sure that does seem odd, but I can assure you that I am no stranger to Libby at this point. Beyond that, she couldn't make this trip to deliver the message herself."

Nils arrives with a mug of hot tea along with a plate containing bits of meat and cheese, but he doesn't set the mug down in front of me yet. Clearly, he intends to be a part of this conversation, as he informs me that he and his wife are not exactly close to Libby. It wasn't a new revelation as Libby had already told me about their estrangement. It was the reason why I first balked at fulfilling Libby's request. Sure, she'd paid for every expense—and even my time. But if I hadn't grown so close to her over these last ten months, there is no way I'd have accepted this assignment.

"Look, I realize all that. I'm not here to do anything but deliver a message exactly as Libby would have if she could have come herself. When I've said her piece, I'd appreciate your hospitality to put me up overnight, and then I will depart quietly in the morning."

Linn glances toward her husband, then back at me with her steely blue eyes. Even her long hair—darkest close to her head but layered on top with silver, grey, and white—looks so much

5

like Libby's. Linn wears it swept up in a bun with a clip to hold it in place, yet pieces of her hair fall from the bun and rest against the sides of her head. Her face even holds many of the same laugh lines and wrinkles as her twin. Even with their similarities, however, I sense a very different spirit in her than that of her sister. There's a hardness that makes her appear paper-thin around the edges, whereas her sister's appearance is soft.

"Okay, Will, we won't shoot the messenger. What does Libby have to tell me?"

"She's dying, Linn. I made the final arrangements for this trip before I really knew just how close to the end she is. In fact, I got a text upon landing that she's been admitted to the local hospital again."

Linn doesn't take her eyes off me, and Nils puts his hand on hers as it rests on the rustic wood table.

"Her message to you is that she has terminal untreatable cancer, and it's in the final stages. But what she really wants you to know is that

6

she loves you, that Jesus loves you, and she wants you to know him before it's too late."

Linn lowers her eyes to stare at the mug in front of her. Nils shifts in his seat before responding for the two of them.

"Thank you, Mr. Westfall. We don't buy into all that religious stuff Libby believes, and she should know that by now, but we appreciate your coming all this way to tell us of her situation."

"I have her handwritten letter to leave with you too."

I reach into the inside pocket of my jacket, pull out the legal-size envelope, and lay it on the table in front of Linn. She simply stares at the thing but never reaches for it.

Nils stands up, gives his wife a peck on the top of the head, then comes around to my side of the table. He holds out his hand, and I take the cue and stand to shake it.

"We're going to bed now. I'll show you to the bathroom and bedroom down here—all yours, as we're upstairs. Feel free to take the tea and food to your room with you tonight. Coffee and pastries in the morning before you leave. Thanks again."

Just as well as I can follow instructions, I know when I'm being given the brush-off. Without another word between any of us, I pad off in my stocking-clad feet to wash up and get some much-needed sleep. I've fulfilled my obligation to her, however poorly it was delivered…or received.

Still dark, I rise to my cell phone alarm at seven in the morning in order to shower, shave, and dress from the few items I brought in my backpack. As I brush my teeth in the small bathroom, my thoughts return to Libby. Is she still alive? I figure I probably slept better in a strange bed in Switzerland than she has in her hospital bed back in Colorado Springs. There's some comfort in knowing that this wasn't new to her. She'd been admitted last month for a few nights before being discharged to return home with regular nursing visits. The cancer had moved from her pancreas to the bone. I'd had an opportunity to learn a few things about her care, even though I was there only a few hours, a couple of days a week.

I leave the small bedroom as I'd found it and shut the door behind me. As I return to the living area where I'd met with Nils and Linn just a few hours earlier, the smell of coffee hits me immediately. I catch a glimpse of Linn in the kitchen when I step toward the table.

"Good morning, Will. Coffee is ready. Would you like some?"

"Sure thing."

"Do you take anything in it?"

"Just straight is good."

"Great. There are pastries in the basket on the table, along with butter and jam. Help yourself. Nils isn't much of a morning person, so you probably said your good-byes last night."

"No problem. I understand."

I sit down at the table and place my backpack on the chair next to me. Linn seems to waltz toward the table and then dips to place the hot coffee in front of me. I want to look over toward the almost visible vista outside the big windows, but instead my eyes are drawn to her movement—even her gait is like that of her sister. However, as I look up to thank her, I'm struck by another difference between them: beyond looking harder than Libby, Linn appears older and more tired—at least until these last few months of disease progression with Libby. Of course, to my thirty-year-old's discernment, any woman over fifty looks old. But these twins were sixty-two, and even I could see a noticeable difference between them.

As she sits down across from me, she sips her coffee and reaches into the basket for a muffin. With the napkin that covers them laid to one side, I get a whiff of cinnamon and see the homemade goodness. I take an empty white plate and try not to dive into the basket and give away how famished I feel. I watch as she cuts her muffin into halves and spreads butter on each, and I follow suit. The moment I take a bite is when she decides to ask questions.

"Will, how on earth did you end up being employed by my sister? Are you some kind of church worker that calls on widows, or are you with a home visiting agency there in town?"

After swallowing hard to push the muffin slug down my throat, I begin to explain that Libby had placed an ad in the local paper for a companion. She'd had me sign a release for background screening, and then I'd spent an hour interviewing with her for the ten-hour-per-week job. It certainly pays well enough at twenty-five dollars an hour. Just what this doctoral student needed at the time to supplement the only other pay I got as a teaching assistant.

"It's weird. That's all I can say. But I'm sure she trusts you. She blindly trusts everyone and then wonders why they end up hurting her."

"I suppose it seems that way to someone who hasn't been alone as long as she has. Remember, her husband died over twenty years ago now."

"That scum. She's so much better off without him and his devil spawn."

If Libby's life hadn't been such a horror, I would have laughed at the attribution to a devil her sister certainly doesn't believe in. Most assuredly, Linn doesn't believe in God. I must admit, I can relate to Linn in her resistance to the faith her sister walks in moment by moment. Even the sneer on her lips is something I understand, though my recollection of those feelings grows dimmer each day in the light of Libby's inner peace.

"I hear the taxi horn outside. Can't thank you enough for your hospitality, Linn. Please thank Nils as well. I best be off."

"Yes. Assure my sister that I got the message. It's about the only assurance I can send along. Be sure to let us know what happens."

"You'll be informed. I'm certain you are listed as the only family contact in her medical records and with her attorney."

Chapter 2

*You were given this life because you were
strong enough to live it.*
—Unknown

The heaviness I feel as I board the plane to
make the trip back home is unshakable.
Although I had assurances again this morning
that Libby was still with the living, it is clear
I am going back to experience her passing.
As I fasten my seat belt and watch the flight
attendants making their rounds, I'm afraid to
make eye contact with anyone. Grateful to have
a seat between me and the guy on the aisle, I
stare out the airplane window and try to make
sense of the last months.

Why do I care so much? To explain that, I should take you back to the beginning.

It was a beautiful spring day in late March of last year when I first rang the doorbell of one Libby Marie Gerster Stamas. The upscale home was in the southwest part of town—definitely out of my struggling doctoral student league. Just walking up the stone path past the brick and wrought iron fencing to the stately home not far from the Broadmoor Hotel, I felt like I should be looking for the service entry instead of standing in front of the white double doors framed in lush green ivy. Everything seemed so perfect in what was often referred to as snob hill. I mustered up the nerve to ring the doorbell and began tugging on the cuffs of my shirtsleeves when the door opened. Not sure if she was paid help or the women who placed the ad, I thought I'd better clarify.

"Good afternoon. Are you Mrs. Stamas?"

"Yes, and you are Mr. Westfall?"

I nodded affirmatively, she invited me in, and I took my first step onto the glassy marble floor of the entryway. She started to lead me deeper in the magnificent home. Mentally, I had sized it up from the exterior to be about five or six thousand square feet.

As I followed from behind, I got my first look at a trim profile with her long silver-gray hair falling haphazardly around her back and shoulders. I guessed she was just about five feet, five inches and approximately one hundred and twenty pounds. I was anticipating a much older woman, though I'm not good at guessing age accurately. I figured Libby was in her sixties but had been expecting she'd look like my grandmother who had short, curly white hair and thick legs and was a bit bent over. None of those things applied here. Libby could have been one of those silver-aged models in a retirement magazine advertisement.

The sitting room we arrived at was to become our meeting place. Oh yes, the interview itself was just the starting point.

"Mr. Westfall, can I interest you in some tea before we begin?"

"Uh, no. I've had plenty of coffee today, thanks."

"I do enjoy a good cup of coffee too—just not after ten o'clock in the morning. Now, let me start by saying that your background check indicates you're a student at the university in town. I must say you hardly look like a young undergraduate. Tell me what you're doing there."

"Right. I finished my undergraduate degree in business ten years ago and then worked for a Texas-based small business consulting group that also had offices in the Springs. During that time, I achieved my MBA. Eventually, I requested a transfer once I set my sights on going to grad school here and left the firm once I was accepted into the program. I'm thirty years old and studying for my doctorate in a business specialty involving entrepreneurial strategy and operations."

"So, you'll come out of this overeducated and under experienced?"

I chuckled at her blunt characterization, and because she was right.

"Let's move on then. I want to explain my expectations for the role of my companion, for lack of a better term. I've recently lost my dearest friend of many years. Her name was Stressa Marie Alduino—my lovely Italian Catholic neighbor. We'd been through much together. These last few months without her have taken their toll on me. I know I can't replace her, but I need someone to interact with, lest I go mad in my solitude. Mind you, I don't have a problem with being alone. I'm just used to having someone I can speak with from time to time."

"I'm sure I can't take the place of your friend, but I'm a good listener."

"I want more than just a listener. Don't get me wrong—this assignment involves no sex. It doesn't even have to involve friendship, as friendship often isn't compatible with money changing hands. But I am seeking someone who can hear my burdens, bear me up, and keep my secrets. Does that frighten you at all?"

"Frighten me? No, I suppose not."

"Likely because you've never had to do much of that kind of thing."

"Of course, I've had friends and relations that require such things. I'm not a blank slate, even if you are twice my age."

I immediately felt the sting of what I'd said and wished I could shove the words back into my mouth and swallow them. I figured the interview was over at this point. Instead, Libby smiled.

"Mr. Westfall, you are to call me Libby, and I will refer to you as Will. We will be on a first-name basis from this point forward, and we'll consider this your first hour of work for which you will be paid twenty-five dollars. Would you like me to show you around the place so you can get your bearings here?"

"So, I'm hired?"

"Yes. You'll hear from my attorney, who will extend a written offer with terms by the end of this week. Are you okay with that?"

"You surprise me, Libby. I thought you'd want to know more about me before making such an important selection."

"Will, later on you may come to understand my confidence in you. For now, I simply need a yes or no."

"Yes. I can visit with you eight to ten hours per week. And I'm happy to take that house tour now."

As she showed me around, I couldn't help but scatter compliments about in each room. Her taste in decor was impeccable, and the place hardly appeared to be lived in. The only marks of habitation were in her bedroom, where there were books, reading glasses, and a few tissues here and there.

When we returned to the entryway to say our good-byes, she held out her slender hand with long fingers to me. I reached for it loosely, only to feel her grip tighten. It was yet another indication that Libby Stamas meant business.

"Good afternoon, Will. As this is Monday and I attend my book club on most Tuesdays,

I hope to see you on Wednesday. We'll need to establish your schedule of visits, based on your academic requirements, of course."

"Yes, I'll put together a proposed schedule and bring it with me on Wednesday. I can be here by three thirty that afternoon."

"Excellent then. Enjoy the rest of your day."

I was still putting on my jacket as I made my way back down the stone walkway into the sunlight. It was about fifty-five degrees, but I wasn't cold. All I could think about was what an easy gig this was going to be. I was thrilled at the prospect of being able to pull down enough to pay the rent between this and my teaching assistant work. Perhaps it was my male ego but counting on my girlfriend's income as a full-time buyer for a large retailer made me feel inadequate. Okay, maybe inadequate isn't the right word. Truth is I felt like I didn't have much leverage in the relationship as Bethany held all the financial cards. At least I'd be able to pay the rent on our little one-bedroom apartment near the university.

It was the first thing Bethany asked about when she got home that night. I was standing in the kitchen staring into the refrigerator when she dropped her keys and purse on the counter.

"Yep, had my interview, and the old lady hired me on the spot!"

We kissed while our cat Lewis performed slalom between our legs. Things seemed to be heating up when she pulled away and began talking about her workday. I returned to rummaging through the cupboards while deciding what to make for dinner.

"We have leftover spaghetti sauce. Want me to make the pasta so we can finish that?"

Bethany shrugged one shoulder in uninspired approval and headed down the hall to the bathroom. Lewis darted into the bathroom before the door closed behind him.

Chapter 3

*The LORD confides in those who fear
him . . .*
—Psalm 25:14a

On Wednesday, I drove the short distance
to Libby's home with the signed letter of
job acceptance. She took the letter and casually
dropped it on the desk in the sitting room where
we got started. She asked me again if I wanted
tea which I declined. She, however, retreated to
the kitchen to make herself a cup. While waiting,
I studied the fixtures in the room. The furniture
was classic stuff with strong attention to detail,
down to the tasseled pulls on the drapes. Sitting
down on the overstuffed couch, I picked up
the remote control from the side table next to

me and pointed it toward the flat screen above the fireplace mantel, with no real intent to turn on the television. The chandelier-style lighting above my head was the next thing to catch my attention as I put the remote back on the table. I then spent some time staring out of one of the two windows that flanked the fireplace but was interrupted when her voice broke in.

"How was school today?"

"Wow, I don't think anyone has asked me that question since my mother would greet me with it in elementary school!"

"You decide—tell me about school or tell me about your mother. Either way, it's a start."

"Okay. I spent the morning doing research for my thesis and then graded undergrad papers this afternoon."

"That's an easier subject for you, isn't it?"

"What's easier?"

"Your day at school is easier to discuss with me than your mother. I understand. It's early, and we don't know each other."

"No, I'm fine with talking about my mother. She's still living, though in a different state. She's living with my sister in Texas because her mind is going."

"Whose mind is going—that of your mother or your sister?"

I laughed out loud before telling her that it was my mother who seemed to be repeating herself and becoming increasingly forgetful. Libby sipped her tea as I tried to explain how my father had passed away a few years back and my sister was closer to our mother.

"Enough about me. I got to thinking that if I'm going to be a good companion, perhaps I should know more about your friend Stressa. Tell me more about your friendship."

"A good strategy on your part. Will, have you ever had a friend who has walked with you through your darkest hours in life? Someone who instinctively knows why you shudder when a reminder arises from the past?"

"Uh, no, I can't say that I have. Is that what she was to you?"

"Yes—and more. She was smart, insightful, funny, and she shared my faith in Christ, though I'm not Catholic. Despite our doctrinal differences, we were kindred spirits, and I can't wait to see her again in heaven. She passed away suddenly of a massive stroke in her home last fall."

"I'm sorry, Libby. Sounds like she was a great friend. It also sounds like I'm not likely to measure up to that standard. Perhaps you need to start by sharing your past with me so that I can at least know what she knew about you."

"She was a great friend. And while you can certainly learn what she knew about my life, without the shared faith there will be many things you won't understand."

I felt the heat rising on my neck at the insult. Intended or not, I took it personally and saw it as a potential threat of attempts to proselytize.

"Libby, I don't know what your faith is— and you don't know mine. Maybe we should start with you telling me about yours. But please understand that I didn't sign up for conversion to your religion. In fact, I'm not much of anything, and I like it that way."

"I know that. I wouldn't expect you to be different than most on that count. That's how I can make such a statement about your ability to understand. By way of example, if you knew anything about Christianity, you'd know that I can't convert you."

"Good. As long as we're clear on that, I'll try to be open to learning about where you're coming from."

"Great, except that it's more important where I'm going to than where I'm coming from. And for me, that's the other side."

"Other side? You mean heaven?"

"Heaven is a place where those on the other side delight. And yes, I'm going there when I leave this side. However, through the years, I've learned a great deal about the unseen world. I prayed for that knowledge and have been allowed to see more and more of that other side as the years have passed."

At this point, I thought perhaps I'd made a mistake to sign up for this job, but her reassuring voice broke in again.

"No, I'm not crazy or demented. However, I can see this is all too much for you right now. I'll have more tea, and we'll discuss some of the household routines and your schedule of visits."

As I reflect back upon my engagement in the household of Libby Stamas, I consider this first encounter to be the most uncomfortable. However, I can also say that I never again felt that level of discomfort. What I can tell you is that during my time with her, I found Libby to be simultaneously gracious and radically fascinating. Being in her home was like being in the dusty attic of a collector, except that she wasn't a collector of things. Instead, it was her collected story, slowly discovered through our conversations, that made her so interesting.

Chapter 4

And when at last you find someone to
whom you feel you can pour out your soul,
you stop in shock at the words you utter—
they are so rusty, so ugly, so meaningless
and feeble from being kept in the small
cramped dark inside you so long.
—Sylvia Plath, *The Unabridged Journals*
of Sylvia Plath

Things with Bethany were a bit tense as of late. I was feeling pressured again. I knew she moved in with me because she was hoping for a long-term relationship, but I wasn't ready for marriage. Somehow it just didn't seem like we'd been together long enough to know if we were right for each other. When she got in these moods, there was definitely a different dynamic at home. She'd pull away more, we'd argue more, and she'd come home from work late more.

On my way up the steps to Libby's front door, I wondered if I should ask for her advice about relationships and women. Yes, that's a great conversation start I figured.

"Afternoon, Libby."

"Good to see you, Will. Come in and help yourself to anything in the kitchen. You know your way around now."

"I think I'd like some coffee. Mind if I make some?"

"No problem, and of course I'll pass. But be a dear and grab me a few of the lemon cookies, will you?"

As I made my way around the spacious kitchen, I speculated that this home must have hosted many dinner parties when Libby's husband was alive. I didn't know anything about him—not even his name. She'd only told me he was dead—a fact she seemed altogether too adjusted to.

The Companion

As I carried a plate of cookies and my coffee to the sitting room, I could hear the television. It was an early afternoon local news program going on about some home invasion in the northern part of town. As I set the cookies next to Libby and went to sit across from her, she reached for the remote to turn the set off.

"Please, don't stop watching because of me. I'm simply here to keep you company, and I want you to feel like you can just live life in front of me," I said.

"Will, I don't pay you to watch television with me, though it might be nice to go to a movie together sometime. No, I want to talk with you. The furrowed brow you walked in with tells me that something is bothering you. What's going on?"

"Furrowed brow? I didn't even realize that I was wearing concern today. You are an observant one."

"I've learned to become so. I only wish I'd developed the skill much earlier in life. It might have saved me much heartache."

"Heartache? Why, Libby, you strike me as content as a dove."

"Those are called mourning doves for a reason—and that's spelled m-o-u-r-n-i-n-g. Their name hasn't anything to do with the time of day."

"Well, learn something new every day. I always thought they were morning—as in sunrise—doves because you wake up to their cooing and they sound so content. But let's get back to the subject of heartache. Tell me about your heartaches, Libby."

"You first. Why the furrowed brow?"

"Brow? Oh, yeah. I guess it's a good subject to broach with you—I could use your womanly advice. You see, I live with my girlfriend. Her name is Bethany, and we've been together a little over six months now. We seem to have developed a pattern of one good month, followed by a tense month . . . then back again."

"So you're having a tense month. Don't tell me—she wants to get married, right?"

"How'd you know? Well, actually, I don't know that she's upset about that. Could be something else. But that's been the usual pattern, so I'm assuming she's bothered about it again."

"Of course it is. She seeks a promise that you probably can't or won't keep. She doesn't yet understand that it is difficult to gain the long-term affections of men because of their tendencies to fluctuant disloyalty."

It was like she'd verbally kicked me in the groin, yet when I looked up from my coffee cup, there sat Libby with her usual lovely smile.

"Are you taking her side without hearing me out? I'm not ready to get married, Libby. We met less than a year ago now. We need more time to figure out if this relationship is right for both of us."

"What is it that you need time to figure out? Whether or not you're sexually compatible? Let's face it, how long could it take to know that you are both able to have sex?"

"No. It's not that."

"You're right. It's not that, because if that's all it was you'd already have your answer. After all, sex is a stark barometer for a relationship, much less a marriage. So if tomorrow she refused to have premarital sex, you'd stay with her because of your deep and abiding love for her, right?"

"That's not fair. I don't think she'd like it much if I refused to have sex with her. It goes both ways."

"Yes, it does. So has she tested you on it? You know—refused sex until marriage in order to learn what's ultimately important to you?"

"Of course not. We don't withhold from each other as a test of devotion. That's ludicrous."

"Is it? Marriage is a promise, and a promise isn't real unless it is unto death—a willingness to die to fulfill it. Christ is the perfect model. He is the ultimate husband to his bride, the church, and a model to all human husbands who must be willing to die to self to keep their vow. Are you ready to do that for Bethany? Or are you just playing house? She has a right to know the truth. The best way to know that is to demand sex only inside of marriage. My guess is that if she laid down such a demand you'd walk away in order to find sex elsewhere, thereby proving that you're only using her."

"Wow . . . that's harsh. I'm not sure I want to discuss it anymore."

"I don't blame you. But, as you say, it works both ways. If you want to know if she's just using you, you too can demand sex only inside of marriage. But my guess is that neither one of you is willing to die to self. And if I'm right, you'll never marry, or worse, it will be a marriage of two selfish people."

"Libby, I said I don't want to discuss it anymore. You've given me your advice; now let's change the subject. Your choice of subject, just not this one."

"Very well. Are you one who enjoys games? I love them—all kinds. Perhaps you'd like to try your hand at gin or canasta—maybe a board game?"

"It's been years since I've played games. You pick one that you think we can finish in the next ninety minutes we have, but you'll have to review the rules with me. No doubt you'll take advantage of me in whatever you select."

"Nonsense, you're an intelligent man who is only lacking in wisdom."

I gave Libby my best frown of disapproval, but she just patted my hand and smiled as she got up from the couch and walked to the small table on the far side of the room. It was near the light of the large windows, and there was already a chess set on top and a chair on each side of the table. I wondered if she'd choose that game. I also wondered if Stressa played games with her. How long had it been since someone had played games with this lonely widow?

"Let's not play this game. This lovely and expensive chess set sits here like an ornament. I detest the game. Would you be so kind as to move it over to the window seat for me, Will? I'll grab some cards."

Once I returned from my chore to sit down across from Libby, I realized this was the closest I'd ever been to her due to the size of the table. Seeing her directly face-to-face in a different light gave me a different perspective on her. I studied the lines on her face and the bend of her hair at her shoulders as she slowly shuffled the cards. The soft, white blouse she was wearing revealed just a hint of cleavage. There was no doubt that Libby still had a killer figure, despite her age. Before I could catch myself, I blurted out the question rolling around in my head.

"You said your husband died over twenty years ago, so why haven't you ever remarried?"

Chapter 5

*A secret weighs on us, a terrible secret
weighs with a terrible weight.*
—**Sue Miller, *While I Was Gone***

I couldn't turn off the thinking machine that
night. As I lie in bed and stared at the ceiling,
my thoughts darted about from Libby's face, to
the card game she taught me, to what she said
about me and Bethany, and to the story of her
husband. But it was the latter that I couldn't
shake. Libby had calmly told me about her
dead husband, Nikolas Yianni Stamas, who
she referred to as Nik. She told me he had died
in 1995 of a heart attack while on business
in Copenhagen. Apparently, Nik was a big-
shot finance executive for a tech firm that had

numerous government contracts at home and abroad. It required him to travel a great deal and even to stay overseas, sometimes for months at a time. I showed interest in his education and background as the guy had his MBA and was also a CPA, but what she really wanted me to know was that Nik had even been a close advisor to their Greek Orthodox bishop. He sounded like quite an accomplished and upstanding guy. But her countenance changed as the story unfolded. In fact, our card game came to a halt, and her eyes filled with tears as she informed me that her husband was not the man everyone thought he was.

"You see, Will, my husband actually died of coital cardiac arrest. However, the truth of his shadow life became known to me only after I received a letter from an attorney in Denmark with a request for money to support his male child who was by then five months old. Of course, I would have assumed a case of mistaken identity had the letter not included the death certificate from that country. I had been told only that Nik died of a heart attack, and I even received an American version of a death certificate with that sanitized information.

"It was his boss, the CEO, who had been the one to deliver the initial news of Nik's demise. He came alongside me for months after Nik's death, telling me what a great man my husband was, even seeing to many of the funeral arrangements and life insurance for me. The cover-up of my husband's many betrayals became known to me only over the course of the following months and years.

"Each discovery was like a stingray barb of pain, penetrating to the bone, laced with poison now embedded in the marrow. With each uncovered lie, I became a vessel of dark secrets as I tried to keep his reputation intact for others. I carried the knowledge of his deceit inside. They were like worms, bugs, venomous snakes, and spiders crawling around my insides. And when they weren't crawling anymore, they died inside of me and left putrid rot in their place. I lived as one held ransom by shame. Even

39

though many didn't know the truth, I still felt like a gazingstock because of that shame.

"I was the sweetheart of Nik's youth, embracing him with arms of love and affiance freely given. In return, I was betrayed and dishonored by the one I trusted most of all.

"Will, for many years I wanted justice for the betrayal, but I know that justice is not mine to execute. I loved my husband and was given to him at an early age, right out of college. It was a bond so strong that even his sham life couldn't completely tear apart the intention of one flesh. I am barely emotionally healed, though I don't blame God because Jesus has loved me like one should be loved: consistently. He alone is faithful and true. I've come to the conclusion that most men see with their brain and feel with their eyes. Furthermore, I've considered that perhaps marriage has become an idol in our society—fool's gold or a mirage. After all, it could hardly be holy matrimony in a broken world that mars the picture of perfection of Christ the Bridegroom and his bride, the

Church. Perhaps, in part, that is why Saint Paul urged staying single."

I shifted in my chair while leaning toward her to say, "I don't know anything about that. I just wonder if you haven't really let go—forgiven, that is."

She leaned toward me such that there were inches between our faces and said, "I have come to a point of forgiving many people in my life, but I also know that an inability to forget has led me to an inability to be glad in this life. But for Jesus."

Then, leaning back in her overstuffed chair and grabbing the wings with her hands, she let out a long sigh. "Will, I now feel like I'm killing time—and that's killing me. I was hoping you could help."

A cold sweat had formed on my upper lip as I lie in bed thinking about her story . . . and her expectations. I used the back of my hand to wipe it away and turned my head to look at Bethany's shapely silhouette in the dark. In an instant, I remembered what Libby had said about my own struggle over the marriage question. Knowing Libby's marital story, I could now justify myself because clearly it must have been bitterness coming through in the form of advice. Surely Libby's experience in love would never be mine. If Bethany and I did marry, it would be because we had explored our compatibility and knew each other inside and out, right?

The following Monday was to be another afternoon with Libby. She wanted me to help her clean out her attic—something that promised to be a weeks-long project. After she showed me the decorative rope that dropped the hidden staircase in the ceiling, I began the climb and then watched her come up the steps behind me. She flipped up the light switch that was mounted on one of the beams next to the hole through which we entered. The attic was big enough that we could stand up, but she asked me to square up both the folding chairs that were leaning up against a dusty antique dry sink. After setting those up, she promptly sat down on one of them.

"You okay?" I asked.

"Yes, just a bit tired today. My goal this afternoon is only to separate out those things that we need to move to the kitchen. I've arranged to have a truck come by in about ten days to pick up things that will go to an estate sale. Maybe we'll just stage them over by the staircase. And, of course, we'll make a separate pile of things to be donated."

I watched Libby drag her chair over to a big trunk where she sat down and opened the lid. She seemed lost in her chore, and I was left standing there.

"What do you want me to do for you now?"

Libby turned her head to peer over her shoulder and then motioned for me to join her by the trunk. I put my chair next to hers, sat down, and stared into a cedar trunk containing all manner of things. There were linens, a box of old Matchbox cars, photos, and more. I reached down deep to pick up a five-by-seven silver frame containing a wedding photo. As I drew it out of the trunk, Libby didn't even seem to react, yet the photo was clearly her as a beautiful bride. The flowing white wedding dress appeared to have a longish train, and the bouquet in her hand looked like white roses. Given the angle from which the photo was taken, I could see her striking dark hair pulled up from her face into a cascade of silky tresses. While I suppose most women would focus on the dress, shoes, and headpiece, I found myself studying the lines of her youthful body.

"Libby, what a drop-dead gorgeous bride you were," I blurted out.

She looked over at me and then patted my knee.

"Thank you, Will. That's very kind of you to say. It was a long time ago and a life that wasn't real."

"What do you mean, not real? You did get married—this was your wedding day, right?" For some reason, my voice sounded a bit desperate.

"Yes, it was that day. And I was full of all the normal bride jitters and excitement about a future together with the man who promised

44

to love me and forsake all others. But it wasn't true. None of it was true. In fact, it was just the opposite. Apparently, he had contempt for me—enough to live a lie for many years. Or perhaps it was just that he loved himself more than anything else. I'll never know for sure because I was never able to confront him with his deception and lies. After trying to deconstruct those decades when I thought I was happily married, all I know is that it started with silences that became secrets that became lies."

I could see tears pooling at her eyelids, and my heart went out to her. After all these years, it was as though she had just learned of her husband's adultery. I had to look away, and my eyes went directly to another wedding photo that was loose in the trunk—one of the couple together.

"Was this him?" I asked as I tried to pull his story out of his dark eyes looking back at me.

"That is Nik. It's the only photo I have retained of him. Through the years, I've destroyed so many in an effort to deal with my pain and anger."

"Libby, I have to say something. I hope you aren't offended by it, but this guy didn't deserve you. I mean, he wasn't just disloyal; he was one homely dude."

She tossed her head back and laughed lightly while brushing away a teardrop that had escaped.

"True enough. He wasn't good looking. I used to believe an average-looking man, or even a homely one, as you put it, wouldn't stray. Now I know that they are even more likely to stray because of low self-esteem, which requires constant reassurances that they are attractive to the opposite sex. Perhaps I'd have been better off marrying a handsome man like you, Will."

"Oh, stop. I wasn't fishing for compliments, just noting that you two seemed a bit mismatched," I said as I turned my attention back to the contents of the trunk with a desire to change the subject. "Say, don't you need some boxes to start sorting into? Do you want me to get some from the university? There are always empty boxes lying around there that I could bring next time I come."

"That would be wonderful. You're right. Let's just sort out the big stuff and worry about these things later. For example, that dry sink and the full-length mirror next to it are going to be picked up," Libby pronounced as she seemed to be caught up in the effort now.

Chapter 6

*I have learned now that while those who
speak about one's miseries usually hurt,
those who keep silence hurt more.*
—C.S. Lewis

By Thursday I had collected enough boxes
of all sizes that would fit through the hole
in the ceiling to Libby's attic. That afternoon I
pulled the car up in the sweeping driveway on
the side of the house and began unloading the
boxes onto the stoop by the service entry. For a
split second, I could relate to the housekeepers
that came every other week to clean for Libby.
It was also where the guy who saw to her
massive grounds would leave his bill and notes
about what was accomplished during his visit. I

noticed she kept a milk box by the door where the local delivery folks would pick up and drop off dairy products every few weeks. It made me smile as I thought about how she took very little tea or coffee with her cream.

As I brought the last load of boxes to the door, I wasn't sure if I should ring the buzzer or go around to the front where I typically entered. No, it wasn't a status thing. After all, I was "the help" so to speak, but somehow, I felt like I'd become more than that. Despite what she'd been through, Libby was a trusting person. I decided to ring the buzzer and waited patiently for her to fetch me.

"You remembered to bring boxes. How thoughtful of you," Libby lilted.

"Of course I remembered. We're going to need these for sorting. I hope you haven't been climbing up and down that ladder alone in this house. It's best I help you as this really is a two-person job."

Libby cast me a sweet kind smile. I'd seen those before. It was her way of saying thank you.

The Companion

I found myself wanting to collect those glances because they were so affirming. It made me wonder why I needed such affirmation. And why would I need approval from this particular woman?

"Shall we get right to it, or do you want to start with afternoon tea?" I inquired.

"Let's get right to it, if you don't mind."

As she handed boxes up to me through the attic hole, I marked them with the words "keep" or "discard" or "donate." Libby and I put in several hours in the attic. She started by asking me about Bethany.

"She's doing pretty well, though somewhat discouraged at work with a newer boss who seems a bit controlling." I looked over to see if Libby was taking all that in, and I could tell she was really asking about our relationship. I glanced down at my shoes before sliding one of the heavier boxes over to the opening.

"Okay, I think she's starting to wonder why I'm not demanding sex."

Libby stood up straight and put her hands on her hips.

"Well, why aren't you?"

"I decided to give your theory a try."

"Wait just a minute. You're not playing straight with her. You're playing a game, and she doesn't know the rules. That's not fair. That's not how it works. She deserves to know your thoughts. I thought the whole idea of living together without benefit of marriage was to get to know each other better."

I hung my head. "You're right. I should have the conversation with her."

"Why do you think you haven't had that conversation?"

"I'm a coward. Honestly, I suspect she'll think I'm strange and walk out of my life," I responded.

"You really need to decide if you're going to set the table for this test. More importantly, you need to decide if you can accept the consequences of her answer. If you don't have the courage of your conviction, then don't bother. Float along as you have been, but don't confuse the poor thing."

The Companion

We finally called it quits around four thirty that afternoon, and as I walked out of the house, I determined to let Bethany know what I was thinking over dinner that weekend.

I probably don't need to tell you that Libby's first question on the following Tuesday afternoon was about how that conversation went. So I told her.

"Bethany thought it was a quaint and old-fashioned idea. She agreed to abstain and appears to be satisfied that I'm further down the road to considering marriage."

Libby looked dubiously over her teacup at me as she sipped but didn't inquire any further.

As we finished up, I thought it was my turn to ask Libby a hard question.

"Libby, if your husband had lived and confessed, would you have forgiven him or left him?"

I detected a slight falter in her voice, as though the question had almost knocked her over. I saw her reach for the chair as if to hold herself steady.

"I will never know the answer to that, Will. Upon finding the truth over the course of months and years, it became evident he was a serial adulterer. Based on what came to light, and each truth cut like a knife, it became clear that he never would have confessed and would have instead eventually been caught. I look back upon our life together, which I thought was good, and realize that I was being ignored. It took years for me to understand that—to acknowledge that the one person I thought accepted, loved, and maybe even cherished me actually rejected, hated and ignored me. I lived with symptoms of post-traumatic stress for a long time. In fact, I'm not even sure how long because I broke and everything about my life had to be rewritten."

By now we had both been seated, and I could sense a physical weakness in her. I looked over at her and asked, "Rewritten?"

"Yes, all that I had known turned out to be a lie. You see, truth hurts, but betrayal hurts each time it is remembered. And each betrayal had to be forgiven. But the darkness knew my worst fears, and it did battle with me on that basis. I struggled for years to forgive. . . . So many years, so many things," she said as her voice trailed off and she turned her head to stare out the window.

I was captivated by her story, and even though I felt like it was probably too much for her, I wanted to know more.

"Libby, does it help to talk about it, such that you hired me to listen?"

Her eyes traveled back to me, and they displayed pain. Now I felt guilty.

"Of course, it's why I hired you. Setting the knowledge of God in our hearts was quite literally a masterful stroke of the divine mind. It sets us up to become fully aware of our real unmet need. Unfortunately, most people initially deny the awareness and then eventually quench it."

"Libby, what is that real unmet need?" I inquired with no small measure of trepidation.

"To know and be known," she responded through her kind smile.

Chapter 7

It's our secrets that make us sick.
—Louise Penny, *The Cruelest Month*

As things turned out, the following week Libby called me to say she'd been under the weather, so I should stay clear and instead concentrate on my studies. She insisted on paying me for not working, for which I was grateful. The entire week was a busy one with teaching assistant duties and meeting with my advisor as the process of establishing my dissertation committee was weighing heavy on me.

But while I didn't have to tend to Libby, Bethany had been a distraction. She came home late Friday night after a "girl's night out" and had been drinking too much. She decided to try to seduce me despite the discussion of the previous weekend. I nearly broke but decided to sleep on the couch and call her on it the next day.

There was no doubt this was a difficult thing—living together while abstaining. I tried to convince myself that it was more like having a roommate. I thought the experiment might cause us to go deeper into more meaningful conversation, but Bethany was just becoming more distant.

"Do you want us to fail?" I asked over coffee the next morning.

"No. I was drunk. Sorry. Tell me again why we're doing this?" she asked in snide frustration.

"I thought we agreed to abstain from sex until we get married, if we decide that marriage is right for us."

"Right. But it's starting to feel like you don't really love me."

"So you equate our having sex with love? Isn't that exactly why we're setting sex aside, so we can determine how deep our love goes?

Remember, if we marry, we'll get old. Who knows, maybe even sex gets old. I don't know. I just know that we need to have something much stronger than sex to hold us together for a lifetime. I think it's called commitment: in good times and in bad, for better or worse."

"Okay. I get it. Just needed my coffee and the reminder. You're right, and I'm glad we're doing this."

Somehow I wasn't convinced. As she reached across the table and patted my hand, I suddenly felt like I was looking at a directionless little girl in front of me. Maybe this whole experiment was working on me more than her. Shaking off the feeling, I determined to keep reminding myself of my own words about commitment. If we couldn't handle this and stay together, then it wasn't really love.

With some of the academic and home front pressures off, I returned to spend a few hours with Libby the following Tuesday afternoon. When I arrived, she answered the door but was in her bathrobe and looking like she hadn't yet recovered from her sniffles.

"Still want some companionship today?" I asked at the door.

"Of course. I'm feeling much better than last week. Come in. Can I make you some tea or coffee?"

"Actually, I've had too much of that today. Make yourself some. Can I use your bathroom first, and then I'll meet you in our room?"

As I made my way back from relieving myself, Libby was smiling broadly and then chuckled as she looked at me.

"What?"

"I'm not laughing at you, but you should know that your fly is down."

Without looking down, I promptly zipped up my pants and sat down. She continued.

"It reminds me of how much I tire of toileting and grooming duties. Such a nuisance. But you are one who can tell me when my fly is down. In fact, you are free to tell me when my emotional slip is showing. And after our last meeting, you may want to, but that's what friends are for."

"No, our last time together was fine. I'm more concerned that you haven't even dressed for the day. That's seems unlike you. Are you really okay?"

"Unlike me? How do you know what is like or unlike me? There's so little you know of me. You don't know how much I've slowed down, how my creative abilities have diminished, how much I've withdrawn from life. And you only think you know why that might be."

"What do you think I think it might be?" I inquired.

"You think I'm just depressed and getting old."

"I don't think you're old . . . but I do wonder about depression. I suppose you'd have reason to be. But didn't you say you'd forgiven him? How long can you hang on to the pain, Libby?"

My question seemed to hang motionless like the drapes on the windows. It seemed like an eternity before she spoke again. So I did what most of us tend to do in such circumstances. I moved to fill the silence.

"Perhaps there's more you need to purge . . . more I need to know. Put the painful moments on me."

She looked over at me with tears forming again.

"I want justice, but I know it's not mine in this life. I loved my husband, Will. Marriage is a strong bonding. God has sustained me and will vindicate me in his time. Yes, I have forgiven my former husband, the other women, and my son, even though none of them ever sought my forgiveness or even understood the concept of forgiveness. It's that I haven't been able to forget."

I was blown away by her raw emotion and revelation. Now it was my turn to sit in silence as she sipped on her milk tea. Taking a deep breath, I regained speech.

"Your son? I didn't think you had any children, Libby."

"I didn't give birth to his son, but my response to the other woman's demand for money was to offer to adopt the child, bring him to this country, and raise him myself. Her name was Abielle. She was a mess—a drug addict, completely unable to take care of the child. So I renamed him and became his mother when he was about nine months old."

"What is his name? Where is he now?" I sounded breathy as I hung on every word of her story.

"I gave him a good Greek name—Dimitrios Stamas. He was called Dima most of the time. He's dead."

Chapter 8

You live out the confusions until they become clear.
—**Anaïs Nin**

On my way home that night after hearing Libby's story, I did something I'd never done before. I lied to Bethany. Not willing to do it in speech, I texted her to say I had to go back to the university to complete some work and would be home late. I got the usual "K" back, so I knew she saw it. I did go back to the university, but it wasn't to complete work. I felt compelled to head to the library to see what I could find from the historical records of Dimitrios Stamas. What Libby told me was like a horror story that completely drew me in.

As I searched the internet, pulling up the electronic records and police reports on the computer screen, I read page after page of the shocking crime story in what was then the sleepier town of Colorado Springs. I knew nothing of it because I had arrived in town only two years ago. It dawned on me that I was only slightly younger than the teen I was reading about would have been, had he lived.

The articles indicated that Dimitrios Stamas had been involved with some heavy drug use. Trouble with school officials had led him to drop out of high school the week before he was at the home of a friend when he killed his friend and an older female—a foreign visitor from Denmark. The police photos clearly indicated the bodies were stabbed multiple times. One of the pull quotes from an investigator said he'd never come upon a more "blood-drunk rampage."

I searched and read for nearly an hour before sitting back in the chair. I was reading the cold factual details of what Libby had just poured out of herself in wracked emotion. She told me Dima had always been a bit of a prevaricator, but she knew she was losing control of him by his senior year in high school. She even mentioned something weird—something about seeing a shadowy spirit in a corner of his empty bedroom one night when he was out way past his curfew. She said the spirit frightened her so much she could feel the hair on her head lift at the roots.

According to Libby, Dima had been an average student up to that point, but something had changed. She wasn't aware of his drug use but wondered about some of the friends he was now associating with. She had also caught him skipping school once to spend time at the very home in which he would eventually murder his friend and his birth mother. Libby had also been unaware of the fact that Dima had found Abielle through an early social media site and had made first contact. The woman had decided to come to the United States to meet him, and he hadn't bothered to tell Libby.

Libby wasn't sure if she ever got all the facts correct in her mind because everything seemed to happen so fast. Dima apparently had arranged to meet Abielle at the home of his friend, telling Libby that he was staying overnight to play video games with friends. The three boozed and drugged for hours into the night. There was also court-revealed evidence that the friend either assaulted or had consensual sex with Abielle, though the news accounts noted that she was a known sex worker in Copenhagen. It was about four o'clock the next morning when police officers arrived at Libby's doorstep to give her the horrible news: two people dead and her son in custody after a neighbor across from the small home had called to say she'd seen a young man face down in her front yard. Apparently, Dima had only made it that far before collapsing. He would eventually admit to the murders, be charged and convicted as an adult despite still being seventeen, and given a life sentence.

Libby visited her son in jail several times within the months after the long and difficult trial. During those visits, Dima snarled at her attempts to get him to repent of sin and meet with the chaplain at the facility. On her last visit, he cut the time short and told her he only wished he'd killed her instead of his "real mother." The following week, on his eighteenth birthday, he was found hanged in his cell.

As I gathered up my things in preparation to leave the library, I picked up my cell phone to check the time. It was late, and I let myself in the apartment, dropped my clothes in a heap, and decided to sleep in my underwear on the couch. Before drifting off, I had an overwhelming sense about how little I knew of Libby's sufferings. Perhaps due to fatigue, I could barely lay hold of that strong feeling again in the morning, but I think I finally grasped how critical was my role as her companion. However, I have to admit that my ability to apprehend that realization ebbed and flowed throughout our time together.

Thursday afternoon I returned to spend it with Libby. I rather expected that we'd pick up where we left off, but she seemed chipper, and I wasn't willing to rip open those difficult emotions again. I thought I'd return to something she'd said early in our acquaintance to get her talking.

"So, Libby, you once said that you've been able to see things on the other side as the years have passed. Do you mean that you understand more or have greater resolution about the past as the years have gone by?"

She took a deep breath as she sat on the corner of the couch with a blanket over her bottom half. I didn't know how she could be cold as it was now approaching Memorial Day weekend, and the weather had been warm and sunny for several days. It took what seemed an eternity for her to respond, but I was determined not to speak next.

"I'm hesitating, lest you think me mad. Give me some time to lead up to my answer so that it might somehow, even faintly, make sense to you.

"The heart is never satisfied with memories, and unresolved pain brings grief. We cannot escape the curse that breathes upon us in this life, but what if we could find satisfaction, even joy, in that which is immovable, faithful, and always true that exists beyond the temporal? What if we could grasp the fact that the central story of life is not our own? Or that the central location of our story is not here? And that the central boundaries are not these? Are you with me so far, Will?"

"Uh, I'm not sure that I am. Perhaps if you continue, I'll catch up," I responded.

"Okay. As you know, I'm a Christian. I do believe that we can and will reap a divine harvest from what we've sown in this life. Put more simply, if we want nothing to do with God, he will grant us our hearts' desire. Conversely, if we do want everything to do with him and the future he has for us, he'll grant that too. So I have made it my purpose for the last twenty years to seek Christ for insights into the spiritual realm. That is because the other side is where real life exists. Spiritually speaking, this side is often more like the walking dead—or zombies, to use a popularized theme from today. Most people can't see that because they think the temporal is all there is."

"Ah, okay. I think I understand what you're saying now. So you aren't seeing into the other side as an explanation of your past but of your future?"

"I suppose that's the best outcome I could hope for in your understanding of this matter," she said.

Once again, I felt mildly insulted, but less so than in the past when she said such things. In part because I really was having to stretch to grasp what she was getting at.

"Well, of course you know I'm going to want to know what kinds of things you see on the other side. Are you able to tell me what the lottery numbers are for tonight?" I asked with marked incredulity. Then I wondered if I blurted that out of an unconscious desire to insult her faith.

Libby smiled her knowing smile and again looked out toward the window.

"Silly man. What good are lottery winnings in a world where such treasure will only be swallowed up?"

"It could also lead to a new car, house, or an education."

"Oh, my dear one, imposters are so much worse than opponents. You believe that those things lead to happiness when one day they are all outdated and disused. If you dare, let your pain and weakness be an argument for prayers and pleadings to see that which awaits you. It's those things which are lasting and satisfying. Does any of that make sense?"

"I'm not sure, Libby. It's all so esoteric. And besides, I don't pray. However, give me an example of what you have seen."

"I could give you a very recent example of what I've learned, but I am not sure it's something you are ready to hear. In fact, I'm still processing its meaning myself. So let me tell you about an example from last year.

"My friend Stressa passed away on a Sunday last year . . . just before eleven o'clock at night. I had spent my morning in church, and I felt a great joy knowing that she and her husband had attended mass and were enjoying their Sunday together. As the day wore on, I had an overwhelming sense that the invisible was drawing near to me and the power of the visible was waning. I wasn't certain why this sense came upon me but simply leaned into it as the day went on. I did lots of praying, which is simply talking to the Lord. I went to bed around nine thirty and was in a deep sleep for about ninety minutes when, suddenly, I was aroused by a flash of light bright enough to sense with my eyelids closed. When I opened them, all was dark, but I knew that Stressa had passed over into real life. It was not a dream, and I was not at all frightened. A peace came over me, and I asked God to give me the words to say to her husband when he got around to calling me. He did, and that call came around noon the next day to tell me what I already knew."

"Lots of people have premonitions, Libby. In fact, plenty of non-Christians have them."

"Of course. What's key is knowing the source of the insight. When they are of God, for whom it is impossible to lie, they are one hundred percent accurate, one hundred percent of the time."

*If you are looking for your solutions
in the physical realm when there is a
spiritual cause, you are looking in the
wrong location.*
—Tony Evans, *Kingdom Woman*

My next visit with Libby wasn't until the following week and was taken up by driving her to a doctor's appointment. On the way home, she asked if I'd stop at an ice cream store where she bought two single-scoop cones, and we ate them in the car. I told her a joke, and we both laughed way too long. She seemed to be in good spirits, and there was something special about this time together. I can't explain it, but for a fleeting moment, it felt like we were both in our teens and the best of friends.

It was now summer and time to get even more serious about my dissertation. I had a lesser load during this semester but would also be conducting a massive survey that would produce the underlying data needed to complete my work. I mention all this because the summer turned out to be a bit of a blur. So much happened in what seemed like such a short time.

In July, Bethany and I were at a Fourth of July picnic with friends. It was one of those pool party events, with most people hanging out in the air-conditioned clubhouse due to the heat. Things had grown increasingly difficult between us. On this particular day, she seemed very distant—chatting up a group of women rather than being by my side. I assumed she just needed some space, until sometime in the late afternoon I saw her talking with another grad student by the pool. It was bothering me, and to make matters worse, she was in her swimsuit by this time.

Bethany had a great body and even seeing her through the clubhouse window I could tell this guy had his eyes all over her. Trying to put it out of my mind, I started up a conversation with one of my professors. We were about three minutes into our discussion when I looked out the window again only to find that Bethany and that fellow were no longer by the pool. They also weren't in the clubhouse.

I excused myself from the conversation to see if I could find Bethany, though I was unable to locate her. Fifteen minutes later they walked into the clubhouse together, but separated, and she came walking over to me. She had a towel wrapped around her bottom half, but for some reason, I was fixated on the fact that her swimsuit bra strap had a single twist in it. It wasn't like Bethany to present anything but perfection in whatever she wore.

"Where have you been? I went looking for you."

"Oh, I met Tim, and we went for a short walk around the property. Do you know him?"

"No, he's in a different program. There are lots of grad students and faculty here, and it's not like I pay much attention to what others are doing."

"You seem to be paying attention to what I'm doing. Are you jealous or something?" she purred in my ear.

"Yes, I guess I am" was all I could muster. I dropped the whole thing, and we left the party about an hour later, but the ride home in the car was silent.

Over the remainder of July, she grew more distant. Telltale signs of her loss of interest were displaying themselves, including coming home later from work more often than before. The worst of it was her attempts to treat me like a pal or a brother.

I didn't discuss what was going on at home with Libby during that month because she seemed to be experiencing some health issues. Remember when I told you that I took her to a doctor's appointment? Well, it was just her primary doctor, and she had indicated it was just her annual checkup. Turns out that physician didn't like the results of some of her blood work and thus began the process of her seeing multiple specialists. Libby would tell me she was feeling just fine, but I noticed some weight loss because she couldn't really afford to lose weight. The last day of the month was her birthday, and given her waning appetite, I decided to take her to dinner at a nice restaurant to see if that would inspire her taste buds. Besides, now I was lonely and didn't want to eat alone. Bethany had left me for Tim, having moved out of the apartment and in with him just days earlier.

As I drove up to the house and parked, I resolved not to tell Libby what had happened since today was to be a happy occasion. Turning off the car, I took in a deep breath and put my forehead on the steering wheel for what I thought was just a minute. By the time I looked up, Libby was standing in front of the car looking at me with grave concern on her face. I knew I was in trouble because she'd demand to know how I was doing. I put on my biggest smile and opened the car door.

"Hello, Miss Libby. You look lovely tonight in that color of green. Didn't you tell me it's your favorite color?"

Her stare bore a hole between my eyes as she stood there clutching her basket-weave purse in front of her.

"You can't fool me, Will. You're talking too much, and you've forgotten that I told you that navy blue is my favorite color. What's wrong? Tell me everything."

"Libby, Libby, Libby," I said as I shook my head and looked at the driveway paving. "I'm fine—it's just that you startled me when I looked up to see you there. Are you ready for that German food you requested?"

"Silly man, I told you I like German chocolate cake, which I suspect is not German at all. However, German food sounds good to me."

Getting the passenger-side door for her, I thought perhaps I had avoided any further discussion about me. I'd quickly turn things to how her day went when I got back into the car.

"How's my birthday girl? Twenty-six today, right?"

"Will, you're even reversing your numbers. You know I'm sixty-two. Besides, if I were just twenty-six, we'd not be having dinner together as I would never be the other woman to Bethany. How are things with you two these days?"

I swallowed hard.

"She left me, Libby."

With both of us staring straight ahead as I drove to the restaurant, there was a long pause before Libby finally spoke.

"It seems the worst blows dealt to us come from those we love."

I ran my hand through my hair as I struggled within myself as to how to respond.

"That's just it—I didn't love her. You were right. Once I was confronted with the thought of commitment to Bethany for the long term, I knew I didn't love her. All we had was the physical. And I suspect she knew it too, but she's off having her thrills with someone else now."

"The spirit in this age is a passive acceptance of everything except deeply held convictions," Libby said when she finally looked over at me. I could feel her caring gaze, even though I kept my eyes on the road.

"It's probably true that I'm not half the guy that Tim is for her," I blurted out in hurt and anger.

Still looking over at me, she began again what I still thought of as her method of comforting. If only I'd been listening to her pearls of wisdom as they spilled out. But instead, I was so wrapped up in myself back then.

"Perfectionism is an adversary, Will. And it's wholly woven from the thread of pride. Besides, you must understand that these days it seems the world wants a domesticated and hairless man. When, in fact, what real women want is a pursuing warrior who is bigger than life. You were behaving as the former with Bethany: shrinking, one-dimensional, and self-centered. Clearly, she is shallow and unaware of what is good and right. I'd say you dodged a bullet."

I parked the car next to the restaurant and got out to open her door. As I opened it, I heard myself say, "Next time, things will be different."

As she swung her legs around to get out of the car, she looked up at me and said, "There are those who know they need God to change them, and those that expect everyone else to change. I am praying you'll be the former."

Chapter 10

Nobody can go back and start a new beginning, but anyone can start today and make a new ending.
—**Maria Robinson**

Landing at O'Hare airport is not something I look forward to due to the layover of three hours. This first leg from Switzerland had been reasonable, despite the crying baby two seats up from me. At least she'd finally fallen asleep in the last hours of the trip. I did too, after spending hours working on organizing my research data so I could finally begin the findings phase of my dissertation. The nearly two hundred pages of material I have to date is a mess. I can feel the weight of having to organize, edit, and submit my final product by year-end. Though I'm not much concerned about my ability to defend it before my committee, it's the written submission that has me stressed. Perfectionism is a problem, and Libby had called it out correctly.

After getting through customs, I grab a teriyaki bowl at one of the food courts and find a quiet table in a corner by myself. I pull out my phone to check for messages, but there are none. I should be home by late afternoon. I figure I'll probably get my car out of long-term parking and drive straight to the hospital to check on Libby before going home.

A small part of me is anxious about her dying without me being there for her, even though she'd already told me she'd still be on "this side" when I got back. It was another one of those glimpses into the future that she claims to have. She calls them favors, and I'm beginning to find myself trusting her on them rather than thinking she's just crazy. All of them except the one about me.

The Companion

I pull out my tablet to project the appearance of being busy, but I can't get my mind off Libby. Here I am in Chicago, remembering it's the location of the corporate headquarters of the company her deceased husband had worked for. I go stream-of-consciousness as I fill my face with bits of food off of chopsticks.

I had once asked her why she had such a hard time getting past her husband's "fling." Yeah, I used that term. It was callous of me, though not intended to be. Libby hit back hard, and the grim reality of his adulterous life came pouring out of her. You see, it wasn't just a one-night stand with a whore for Nik. He had kept Abielle in an apartment in Copenhagen so she'd be available to him when he was there on extended business. And here in Chicago, it seems he had had an ongoing relationship with one of the executives. Her name was Mellie Summers—a married woman herself. Libby learned of this affair at the same time she learned Nik had also been having sex with his assistant in the local Colorado Springs office.

Her name was Stacy Jones—a young, poorly educated, and promiscuous divorcée. So much so, that word of her promiscuity had travelled even after Nik's death from someone who knew someone who knew Libby's friend Stressa. All of it was so ugly that when I heard Libby refer to her former husband as "weak whore bait," it made complete sense to me.

Let me take you back to that day. It was in late summer, and the heat was really bearing down on our part of the world. Libby and I spent our time in her temperature-controlled home, except for the three-day period when the air conditioner went out and I had to help her get it repaired. I was pretty worried about her overheating as sometimes the elderly do without complaint.

"Libby, do you have anything besides that small fan you keep in your bedroom?" I yelled from the other room.

"Yes, but it's in the garage—a box fan, though I can't quite remember where it is now."

The Companion

As I walked into the sitting room to hand her a glass of iced tea, I told her I'd go find the fan and bring it in. While I was rummaging around in the hot garage, it struck me how big and empty it seemed with just Libby's white Lexus inside. In fact, it made me wonder again why she stayed in this big house for all these years. It wasn't just the upkeep, but how could it not be a terrible reminder day in and day out?

I spotted the fan sitting near the water heater. It had spider webs on it but appeared to be nearly new. As I returned through the mudroom, I stopped to wipe the fan down with a paper towel and then carried it to where she was now a bit splayed out on the love seat.

"Okay, let's plug this in. Did the repair guy say when he'd be back with the part tomorrow?"

"Oh yes, he was very specific. He said sometime between nine a.m. and four p.m." Libby answered with a smirk.

"Right. Well, I hope it's sooner rather than later. I'm worried about you being alone in this house when the temps tomorrow may be worse than today. Speaking of this house, it's been years that you've lived here. Why didn't you sell and get a smaller place . . . or a place that didn't hold memories of Nik?"

"Perhaps because I love this place, and to the best of my knowledge, he never brought a woman here. If I had discovered he had asked evil to walk in the front door, I probably would have sold it, but I never found any evidence of that."

"But certainly you must have found other evidence of his infidelity in this house," I spoke in quiet prompting. I have to admit, after months of working for and knowing Libby, I had come to realize how much I had initially discounted her story and her pain.

"I found plenty. It came layer upon layer. They sent me his belongings, including his cell phone. I figured out his passcode, and there they were. Message upon message from other women. I didn't know about them, and they didn't know about each other. Unfortunately, I was the one who had the shame of bearing his last name. The hardest to hear were voice messages from calls that were made on my birthday or our anniversary. In fact, it was our last anniversary together on which he called to say he had to work late. I had worked all day to make a special dinner, a dinner I ended up eating alone, but I believed his excuse. I later found a receipt in a suit pocket from that very day . . . for women's lingerie that I never saw.

"It took several years to reconstruct what was really going on, but I was determined to rebuild the entire mess, based on what was actually happening instead of the fake world I lived in. It was important because immediately after I learned of his affair and child with Abielle, I felt like a woman with no past. Everything I had believed was a lie. There are even places I can't go now because I know he took another woman there."

"Go on. I'm listening, but continue only if you are up to it," I said.

"I looked back and learned that I was dishonored and affronted at almost every turn without even realizing it. As I've told you, it's hard to acknowledge that the one person you thought accepted, loved, and maybe even cherished you, actually rejected you. I broke, and all things had changed forever. I had to start over."

I scratched my head and must have had a screwed-up look on my face because she asked me what was wrong.

"Then I'm even more confused as to why you would stay in this house and sleep in that—" I caught myself before I said it, but she finished the sentence.

"—bed? It's a logical question. First of all, I had all the furnishing replaced or rearranged. I even had the master bathroom remodeled. Believe me, I never think of him in that way anymore, because it would just make me feel dirty. No, he had taken everything else from me, but I wasn't about to give up my house. Home is important to a woman, Will. Did you know that?"

"I'm afraid I don't know much about women at all, Libby. Probably never will."

Chapter 11

You and I will meet again
When we're least expecting it
One day in some far off place
I will recognize your face
I won't say goodbye my friend
For you and I will meet again
—**Tom Petty, "You and I Will Meet Again"**

I showed up at my appointed time the following week after the air conditioner was fixed. As usual, Libby answered the doorbell at the front entrance. I was not a few steps into the house when she exclaimed, "What is that awful smell?"

I looked down at my shoes to see if I'd stepped in dog poop or something, but nope.

"What smell? What does it smell like to you?" I inquired.

"It smells like cigar," she responded with her hands on her hips.

"Oh, I didn't realize you could smell that."

"Have you taken up smoking cigars?"

"No, Libby. I don't really like them much myself, but I endure them at my new assignment."

Instead of letting me pass, she stood scowling right in front of me with her arms folded across her chest.

"What new assignment?"

"Without Bethany's income, I need to take up another part-time job. I found a family that needs me to do the same for an elderly man who lives not far from my apartment. He happens to smoke cigars from time to time. See, I've become a professional companion!" I chuckled over that last comment, but she wasn't budging.

"I don't want to share you, especially with someone who smokes. You'll be showing up smelling like that awful weed. No, I won't have it. You'll need to leave."

"Libby, don't be ridiculous. I'll figure out a way to do my visits with him on alternate days from yours if that will help."

"I'm not being ridiculous. I'm being picky. I insist on paying your full rent in order that you might cease working for anyone else but the college."

"I'll consider that and get back to you. Are you sure you want me to leave? I'll come back tomorrow afternoon if you like."

"I would like that very much. After you've been out of that man's space and had a chance to shower. Mind you, your clothes will start to smell like him too. Oh, Will, please do consider my offer."

I did return the next day, smelling fresh and even wearing a splash of cologne. It was something Bethany had bought for me at my last birthday, though I don't go in for that kind of thing much.

This time Libby greeted me per usual, and we made our way to the sitting room where she was already consuming her afternoon tea. Once I was seated, I asked her what she'd like to discuss today.

"Yesterday, of course."

"Oh, you mean you expected a decision from me today?"

"Yes. How long does it take to consider my offer and tell the family they'll need to get another sitter?"

"Sitter? Is that what I am to you, because I certainly don't think of our many months together like that at all?"

"No, I consider you my friend. And I suppose I am jealous of our limited time together," she said, looking downcast. The afternoon sun through the paned windows cast streaks of light across her sadness.

"I see. Are you saying that you want me to be exclusively visiting with you, or are you open to altering our schedule a bit to accommodate separate days with the old guy? He's really quite harmless. Likes to play gin and needs someone to make up some meals and tidy up around his place."

Libby stared off into the distance and then mumbled something I didn't catch the first time.

"What was that?" I leaned forward to ask.

"My husband smoked cigars whenever he could get away with it."

"Huh. So, I guess it brought back a bad memory for you then. Is that it?"

"I hate the smell."

We sat in silence for a few minutes, and then I assured her that I'd drop the second job and appreciated her offer to pay my rent.

"Thank you, Will. Though I know that I am fully able to trust Jesus, there is in me an overwhelming drive toward wanting to be known by another human being."

"I am struck by how you seem to know God, and I must say that I've wondered why you would need a companion if God is so great a friend," I admitted.

"Yes, he calls me friend, but I call him King. It doesn't mean he's not approachable, but it's quite different to have an earthly friend. I suppose Stressa played that role for so many years, but now she's gone to be in the presence of the King. But through you, my companion, he lays his healing hand upon me."

In an instant, I understood how important I had become to Libby. It was simultaneously gratifying and frightening—almost a burden too great to bear. Yet I sat there knowing that I was in the presence of someone who had been crushed in life, and I wanted to be there for her.

"I hope I can bring you some healing, Libby. I know this life has dealt you a bad hand."

"Oh my. I don't think of life as a game of chance. I believe all things work for good to those who love Jesus. Furthermore, there is a virtue in hardship, Will. The virtue of hardship is fortitude, but every virtue has an enemy, and the enemy of fortitude is resignation. You are helping me fight that enemy. And any inanition is dispatched because of Christ Jesus."

"Okay, tell me more about this Jesus and his purpose for your life." I could hardly believe I was asking such a question. But when I look back on this conversation, I know now it was the stuff of quatervois.

"My belief is so strong that even my Lord had placed me on this earth to say or do something that led just one person into heaven, I would be content for having lived a life with that single purpose before me," she responded as the sun now shone fully on her face.

I could hear the disbelief in my voice as I asked, "Am I that one person, Libby?"

"Now you are moving into territory I have told you about before—those things that he sees fit to share with me. But I want you to know that they are never quite that clearly defined. He shows me things that require some discernment beyond what I am shown."

"Has he shown you something about me?" I asked after swallowing hard.

"Yes. Are you certain that you want to know it?" she inquired looking directly into my eyes.

"Yes, even this skeptic wants to know."

"He showed me a glimpse of you greeting me in heaven, Will."

With great relief, I exhaled audibly. "That's probably very reassuring, and if there is a heaven, I'm sure it will be a great reunion of friends."

"There is a heaven, but since your discernment isn't currently for the things of God, you may have missed the revelation in this vision. You see, Will . . . I am old, and you are young, but it is you who will greet me upon my arrival."

Chapter 12

For death is no more than a turning of
us over from time to eternity.
—**William Penn**

I must admit, I was totally discombobulated for days after that last meeting with Libby. Her revelation made little sense to me, yet I couldn't get it out of my mind. And while things were gearing up again at the college for the fall semester, I felt distant from the work at hand. I couldn't afford to be distracted as I was now coming into the home stretch of my doctoral program.

The first Monday in October I was to drive Libby to another doctor's appointment. She had not been feeling well but would admit to only general malaise and fatigue. However, I noticed that she looked even thinner when I picked her up that day. Switching from my own car to drive her to the appointment, I backed hers out of the garage and saw her through the rear windshield looking gaunt under a dark shawl she had wrapped around her shoulders. When I put the car in park and jumped out to help her into the passenger side, I caught a whiff of her perfume. It was the same scent she always wore, but I'd never asked her what it was, so I started the conversation there.

"Libby, what is that perfume you always wear?"

"Oh dear, you can smell that? Is it too strong?" she asked with concern showing in her eyes. In an instant, it occurred to me that her eyes were her favorite color—navy blue.

"Not at all. I've just been catching the scent for all these months, and it took me this long to mention it."

"It's called The One. Do you like it?"

"Yes. It seems to fit you, or perhaps it's just that it's become the scent I associate with you," I responded.

As we drove to the other side of town, I attempted to get her to tell me what her symptoms were and what she was seeing the doctor for. She was veiled in her responses, but after waiting patiently for her in the waiting room, she finally decided to talk on the drive back home.

"I've been given a difficult diagnosis. It's my pancreas apparently."

"What about it?" I begged her to go on.

"It is cancer and inoperable."

It was all I could do to keep the car on the road—so much so that I finally pulled over into a grocery store parking lot and shut off the car. After turning toward her, I just stared because words had fled from me.

"I don't want you to worry, Will. We all die, and my time will be coming soon. I do hope, however, that I'll be able to see you get your diploma in the spring. The doctors don't seem to think I'll make it through the winter, but we'll see. I had hoped you'd be willing to walk with me through this valley of the shadow of death, but I understand if you can't. I am not frightened as my darkest gloom shall give place to a morning because Jesus is faithful to carry me if I will simply lie in his arms, desiring only his will."

Running my hand through my hair, I tried not to appear impatient with Libby.

"Is it his will that you should have cancer and die? I don't get that, Libby. What kind of God is that?"

She turned away and stared out the front windshield not uttering a word.

"I'm sorry, Libby, but this isn't going to be easy because I have come to appreciate your friendship. And on top of this news, I have to work around all these myths you believe in. How can you reconcile disease and pain with this God of yours? Of course I'll walk with you through this. I'll be there every step of the way for you, even if it means deferring my dissertation and graduation."

"I won't hear of that. I want you to proceed as normal, though I may be incapacitated on some days . . . certainly in my last days. Do you really consider the gospel to be myth, or is that just something you've concluded out of poverty of research?"

She had me there. I had to admit that neither I nor my agnostic and atheist friends had even bothered to crack open a Bible to know what we were rejecting. But she continued.

"If myth, then poorly written myth as it reads like recorded history, with accounts from those who witnessed a collision of the temporal with the eternal. That's what I want you to see Will; this life is not all there is. The other side is where I'm going, and that is where real life exists. It's where all things will be made new, and I will be truly free. I think it was Robert Frost who once said that the only certain freedom is in departure. I will depart for my real home—that which I am fitted for."

Once again, I didn't know what to say, so I started up the car and drove her home. When we got inside, I immediately started doting on her like a nurse. She noticed and called me on it.

"I'm fine, Will. Let's just have some afternoon tea and play a game or something."

I recall that in that moment I wanted so much to be able to tell her I was praying for her, just as she had so often indicated she did for me. But of course, I couldn't say that with any meaning behind it because prayer was not something I knew anything about. It would have sounded so trite to her... just as it used to sound to me months earlier.

We spent the next hour playing a board game in which Libby trounced me. I think it was because her pronouncement from days earlier reentered my mind, and I kept wondering what the implications were for me, given her diagnosis. She never brought it up, leaving me to wonder if she was rethinking it herself, in light of the fact that she had been given a death sentence. The more I pondered the idea of her being gone in a few months and that meant her "vision" would have me gone even sooner, the weirder the whole thing seemed. I wrote the whole thing off to her illness and my paranoia.

Admittedly, I feared death. Who doesn't? Actually, Libby didn't seem to fear it at all. I think she might have been somewhat fearful of pain, but certainly not death. All I knew is that I wanted to concentrate on being the best companion I could be to someone who was living out their last days. However, my fear was that I'd fail in that effort. I was scared.

Chapter 13

As long as you live,
keep learning how to live.
—**Seneca**

I arrived at the house around one o'clock in the afternoon and found Libby had prepared lunch for the two of us. Perhaps because I didn't usually get there that early in the afternoon, she thought I'd be hungry.

"I really appreciate your thoughtfulness, but I've already eaten."

"Well, sit down and pretend then, Will. I've been eating alone for so many years of my life, and I'm so tired of it. Just go along with it," she insisted.

"Of course. These cookies look pretty good. I didn't actually have dessert when I ate lunch."

105

"What's new?" she inquired as she sipped on her iced tea before starting in on the chicken salad.

"The cat died in the night. I had to drop off his body at the shelter this morning and pay an incineration fee."

"What cat? Did you tell me you had a cat before?"

"No. You aren't forgetting things. I never mentioned it. Lewis was a gray tabby that Bethany brought to the relationship. He was never a very healthy thing, and Bethany apparently couldn't be bothered with him anymore. She didn't take him with her when she left me this summer. I did my best to keep him comfortable this past week, but when I woke up this morning, I found his body in the closet. He had tipped over my laundry basket and crawled in there. Poor old guy."

"I'm sorry to hear that. You should have told me. Why didn't you tell me?"

"I suppose I didn't want to burden you. I also thought that perhaps you'd feel the same way about cat dander as you do about cigar smoke."

"No. I like animals. I had a small dog for about ten years. Her name was Clara. A bit yappy, but she was good company most of the time. Unfortunately, Dima never seemed to like her, so I had to keep them apart."

"Let's talk about something more pleasant. What should we do for the holidays?" I asked.

"Holidays? You should be going home to see your mother in Texas, of course."

"No doubt I'll do that at Christmastime, but what do you say we do something together for Thanksgiving? We could cook up something in your big kitchen, or perhaps we might go find a poor man's turkey dinner at Denny's and eat that!"

Libby laughed out loud as she reached for a cookie. It was good to hear her laugh.

"I like the idea of not having to cook. Heck, we could even pick up the whole meal at the grocery store and bring it home. I could set a pretty table, and we could just pretend we made it ourselves."

The Companion

By the time Thanksgiving rolled around, Libby was just too ill for cooking or even picking up food. We ended up going to Denny's, though she really didn't eat much besides mashed potatoes and cranberry sauce.

I had planned to drive down to Texas to stay at my sister's for about a week during Christmas, but that was cut short by a day when Libby texted me from the hospital. She'd had a pretty rough few days, and the doctor admitted her over the holiday for what ended up being not much more than trying to get fluids in her, adjust medications, and general observation. There was no doubt she was getting weaker.

When I returned from my holiday trip, it was to pick her up at the hospital and drive her home. It was a good opportunity to talk to her about increasing her in-home nursing visits and other discharge instructions. It was that evening that she seemed desperate to ask me to return the next day because she had a favor to ask of me.

Pad Brotherton

The earliest I could arrive at Libby's was around four o'clock in the evening. The evening home care assistant was there and had prepared enough dinner for the two of us. We ate dinner in Libby's bedroom, where she sat up in bed, and I had my plate waiting for me on the dresser. Sitting down in the comfy chair not far from her bed, we ate and talked about my trip because she claimed her holiday was so boring. After about an hour, she told me she was getting tired, so I began to gather up the plates to take back down to the kitchen.

"Will, there's something I need you to do for me. It's a big ask, but I'm hoping you'll say yes. It's a bit strange, so bear with me."

"Strange? I'm here for you, so ask away," I said, while staring at her half-eaten meal still on the plate.

"I want to fly you to Switzerland to deliver a letter to my twin sister who lives there. You know, Linn? I think I've told you a bit about her."

"Wow, are you concerned about mail delivery? Why do you need me to do this in person?"

"It's not the mail service. I'm not even asking this because I think I'm going to die any day now. It's just that I've another message from the other side. It's a strong sense that only you can do this. I don't really know why. I am willing to pay for your flight, and I'm sure they'll put you up for the night. If you want to do sightseeing after that, I'll even pay for your hotel stay. However, I know that may be difficult for you to do, given your schooling and such. I do hope you'll do this last thing for me."

"Last thing? So you do think you're going to die soon? I think that would make me very nervous to be gone halfway across the world knowing you might be gone when I return. Is there something else besides the letter you want me to take to her?"

"No, just that and a verbal message I'll give you for her. I'll contact her and her husband, Nils, to let them know to expect you. I'm not sure when you can go, but it should probably be within the next three to four weeks . . . sometime in January. Weather's not great during that time, but that's not really the point."

"Let me look online tonight for round-trip fares and check my schedule for the next quarter at school. Things are easing up a bit in terms of my program because I'm coming into the home stretch on the dissertation. We'll talk about it when I see you next."

Like a plea, she asked when that would be.

"Today is Wednesday, December twenty-eight. I will be back to see you on Friday around two o'clock or so. Do you need me to bring anything with me?"

"Just some peanut butter cups. The home health people won't give me anything that isn't healthy. Sneak some of those in, will you?"

"Of course I will. I bet I can still find bags of those dressed in red and green for fifty percent off now. I'm going to leave your phone on your nightstand here. You feel free to text me any time of day or night."

Chapter 14

There are far, far better things ahead
than any we leave behind.
—C.S. Lewis

I woke up on Friday morning to a text from Libby. It simply said John 3:3. Of course, she knows I haven't been near a Bible in decades, so I had to Google it. Back in Sunday school days, of which I had very few, I remember the teacher telling us that the red letters were quotes from Jesus. The verse was one of those in which he said that no one can see the kingdom of God unless they are born again.

Normally, I would have been agitated by receiving such a message, but it actually didn't affect me that way that morning. I read it several times and send her back a smiley face. That's all I knew to do because I had already determined to bring it up when I saw her in the afternoon. Why shouldn't I let her talk about what was important to her during what were her last months, weeks, or perhaps days? There was something special about Libby, and I felt like she was my own personal secret.

After being at the campus library for about six hours, I made my way to Libby's house. The home care staffer wasn't there yet as she came only in the early morning and early evening. Libby had given me a key to her place so I could let myself in. That seemed like such a milestone because it signaled to me that she truly trusted me.

When I reached the door to her bedroom, I could see her coming out of the bathroom in her white cotton gown that covered her to the ankles. She looked positively ethereal. I cleared my throat, and she looked over a bit startled, while quickly slipping back into bed.

"I am feeling a bit better today, Will."

"So glad to hear that. When does the aide show up this evening?"

"Why? Are you hoping she'll send up room service again?" Libby chirped.

"No, silly. I was just wondering how much time we have before we are interrupted. By the way, I found a few bags of those peanut butter cup candies that you requested. I'm going to put one in the nightstand drawer and one in your dresser drawer. How's that?"

"Wonderful!"

As I dropped the second bag in the top drawer of her dresser, I noticed her pretty lingerie there and the smell of sweet perfume that arose from a heart-shaped sachet in the corner.

"I thought we could spend some time talking about that Bible verse you sent me today. What was that all about?"

"Oh, I do hope you weren't offended. Though actually, the words of Christ are typically offensive to those who are perishing."

"Am I going to perish?"

"We are all eternal beings. Perishing refers to those who will die with no hope because they have rejected the free gift of salvation provided by the death of God's son on the cross as payment for our sin. I only sent it because I don't want you to perish. I want you to share the kingdom of God with me."

"I would like to know we'll see each other again where we could continue getting to know one another," I heard myself say.

"Oh yes! And it will be so much better as we'll be young and healthy—full of joy. He even promises that before we call, he will answer; while we are yet speaking he will hear. That means we'll not only know each other well, but Christ, who knows our needs, will dote on us as we worship him."

"I thought he was supposed to hear us and answer our prayers now."

"He does. However, our requests are not always in his will or aligned with his plans. Most of the time, we are calling to him out of selfish or wrong motives. That's just the nature of this broken world. But one day, all things will be made new, and we'll buzz in complete harmony," she said with a most radiant countenance.

"It does sound wonderful. So was he talking about our being born again when we get to heaven?"

"No, that can happen only this side of heaven. He was talking about a spiritual birth into the kingdom of light which occurs the moment we trust Christ."

"I see."

"Do you?"

"Don't get so worked up, Libby. You've gone from looking so happy to looking so concerned. I meant that I understand a bit better now. I promise to think on what you've said. Now, how about we get into those candies and spoil our dinner?"

Her face lit up as she slowly opened the nightstand drawer. I pulled up a chair, and we ate a few in silence.

"If I feel this good tomorrow, I shall get dressed for the day. I do hope that's the case."

"Me too, though you might want to save up your strength for when I come back on New Year's Day. If you feel pretty good, I'll make some popcorn, and we'll watch a movie on the television. If you feel very good, I'll take you to the theater for popcorn and a movie. What do you think of that?"

Her eyes widened like a child on Christmas morning as she nodded in agreement.

"By the way, I did some checking on airfare to Switzerland, and it looks like I can get out and back cheapest by going during the week. Since I'm on winter break, I could make this trip next week. Will you have your letter ready, and do you still want me to go?"

"Yes, the letter will be ready when I see you on New Year's Day. Go ahead and book your travel, and I'll write you a check to cover that and other expenses."

"That reminds me, my landlord tells me you've paid my rent for January already. Thank you. I want you to know how much I appreciate all the financial support you have provided this struggling grad student, Libby. But I also don't want you to worry about me. I'll be okay. I'm more concerned about leaving you, even for a few days next week."

"You're welcome. I'm not worrying about you. I just wanted to make sure January was taken care of."

"Are you thinking that you won't make it through the month? I hope you're wrong."

"I'm thinking that we shall see Jesus soon. Now that is real hope."

"We? Oh, right . . . you still think I'll go before you," I said with a big grin on my face. "At least my bills will be paid up."

Chapter 15

I see Heaven's glories shine, and faith
shines equal, arming me from fear.
—Emily Brontë, "No Coward Soul is Mine"

We did bring in the New Year at the movie theater. I am pretty sure Libby told me she was feeling better than she actually was. It was some kid movie that had an adult appeal. We laughed, and she ate some popcorn from my hand, rather than getting into the bag herself. She also complained of being cold, even though I had thrown my own jacket over her legs as she wore hers throughout the show.

I really was dreading getting on a plane to Switzerland and leaving her. Yes, I was afraid she'd die while I was gone. That meant I wasn't even sure what to say when I brought her back home after the movie. I hung around a while to make sure the home health aide was tending to her needs. Once she was put to bed, I went into her room, somewhat hoping she might have already fallen asleep. However, she was wide awake and thanking me for the outing again. She said it was almost like we went on a date. That would have seemed awkward to me, even just a few months earlier, but for some reason, not so much at this point.

I patted her hand and told her I'd return as soon as I took care of her request. Though her skin was getting sallow and her cheeks looked a bit sunken, she seemed radiant when I said that.

But that didn't keep me from dreading the assignment I had just carried out for her.

So on this day, I'm not really eager to tell her how her sister had stiff-armed her message. And, as it turns out, I don't have to. Upon my return to Colorado Springs, I drive directly to the hospital from the airport. Libby had been readmitted, and her condition was listed as grave.

I make only one stop before heading to her room, though my stomach is growling and I'm feeling the light-headedness that accompanies low blood sugar levels. I go to the small hospital chapel. I can't tell you why, but I feel absolutely drawn to it like a magnet. Alone I sit for what seemed like forever but was probably only a few minutes. My stomach stops rumbling, and I feel the need to confess my weakness to Libby's God, and ask for his strength in what I'm going through. I even tell him that I trust him with her, and with my own life. After all, she'd portrayed her Jesus as being so kind, it just makes sense in this moment to put my trust in him. I could deal with what that meant later . . . after she was gone. After I lost my companion.

I rise from the uncomfortable chair in the chapel and make my way to the floor and the room where she lies motionless and asleep. I don't know anything about dying, so I'm not even sure she's still alive. The nurse had already informed me that her bodily functions are starting to shut down, and she would be in and out of consciousness and is on pain meds. It's clear to me that she had but minutes to hours remaining.

I hold her hand as I sit in the chair next to her bed. After a few minutes, Libby opens her eyes and smiles with what must have taken all her energy. Then she speaks in a whisper.

"I wish to be unburdened from this life. I wish for the bonds of this world to be loosened. I have finished the race. Thank you, dear one."

Fighting the tears in my eyes and the stinging sensation on my whole face, I finally gather up the courage to speak.

"Look for me in heaven, Libby. I love you and believe in the one you have spoken to me about—your Jesus."

"I know," she says, as her chest heaves and she closes her eyes.

I kiss her dewy forehead, believing she has passed to the other side. My stomach starts growling again, and I robotically walk out of her room, down the hall, into the elevator, and out the front doors of the hospital. I feel like

I'm dissolving into the dark fog of night. I wonder how I can be hungry at a time like this. Everything, even my physical being and my thoughts, seem so surreal.

At the intersection, I pull out my phone and see it's 7:29 p.m. I look up from my phone and see a car run the red light in the intersection. It rams into another vehicle and sends it flying in my direction. I freeze with the realization that there isn't time or space to escape.

Hospital Logs

William Stanton Westfall:
Cause of death: accident; skull fracture
Time of death: (DOA) 7:40 p.m.
Libby Marie Gerster Stamas:
Cause of death: carcinoma of the pancreas
Time of death: 8:22 p.m.

Morgan James makes all of our titles
available through the Library for All
Charity Organization.

www.LibraryForAll.org